by Robin Wasserman
Illustrated by Duendes del Sur

visit us at www.abdopublishing.com

Reinforced library bound edition published in 2013 by Spotlight, a division of the ABDO Group, PO Box 398166, Minneapolis, MN 55439. Spotlight produces high-quality reinforced library bound editions for schools and libraries. Published by agreement with Warner Bros.-A Time Warner Company.

Printed in the United States of America, North Mankato, Minnesota.
102012
082013
♻ This book contains at least 10% recycled materials.

Cover designed by Madalina Stefan and Mary Hall
Interiors designed by Mary Hall

Library of Congress Cataloging-in-Publication Data
This book was previously cataloged with the following information:

Wasserman, Robin.
Search for Scooby snacks / by Robin Wasserman ; illustrated by Duendes del Sur.
p. cm. -- (Scooby-Doo! Picture Clue Books)
[1. Rebuses. 2. Dogs--Fiction. 3. Mystery and detective stories.]
PZ7.W25865 Se 2000
[E]
                                            2001272075

ISBN 978-1-61479-039-6 (reinforced library bound edition)

 and his friends were

camping at the 🏔 .

The ☀ was bright.

There were no ☁ in the sky.

"Like, this is fun, but I'm

hungry!" 🧑 said.

The 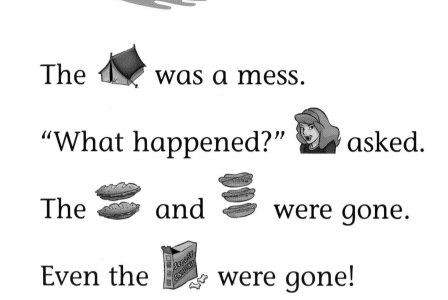 was a mess.

"What happened?" asked.

The and were gone.

Even the were gone!

"It looks like a  did this," said.

"A ?" asked.

"Oh, no!" said . He hid inside the .

"Ruh-roh!" said . He hid under a .

"We need to look for clues," said.

"It is the only way to find the missing ," said.

was scared. But he was also hungry.

"Let's go find that and get our food back!" said.

found a clue.

She found big .

 thought they looked like

monster .

 found a clue, too.

She found her on the

ground.

"Jinkies!" said. "I have a

hunch about who took our

food."

, , and 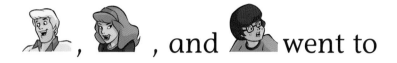 went to

get Park Ranger Adams.

 and sat on a  .

"I wish that I had a 🥧 ,"

🧑 said.

🐕 wished he had some 📦 .

"Like, all this waiting is making

me hungry," said.

"Let's go find some food!"
 shouted.

used his to find the

.

His led him to the .

Then his led him to a deep,

dark .

Scooby looked in the  .

Maybe there was a or a

 in the cave.

"Maybe the are in the

 ," said.

 went into the .

There was a big pile of food,

and the were on top!

Then  heard a noise.

Was it the ?

It was not a .

It was a big, brown .

"Run!" and shouted.

ran away.

But the grabbed 's tail.

The 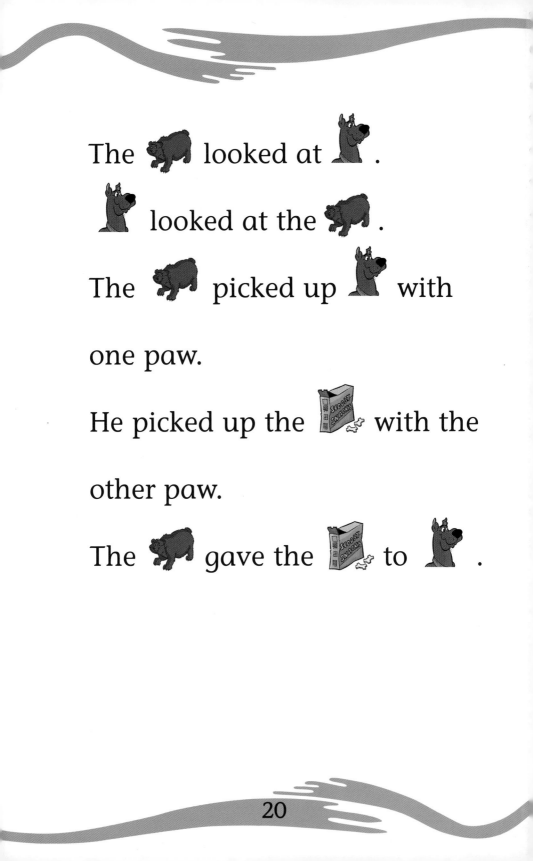 looked at .

 looked at the .

The picked up with

one paw.

He picked up the with the

other paw.

The gave the to .

 brought the gang and

Ranger Adams back to help.

But did not need any help.

"Looks like we found our ,"

said.

"And found his ,"

said.

"Scooby-Dooby-Doo!"

barked.

Did you spot all the picture clues
in this Scooby-Doo mystery?

Reading is fun with Scooby-Doo!